Until The Morning

Alve Jane Aranton

Ukiyoto Publishing

All global publishing rights are held by

Ukiyoto Publishing

Published in 2024

Content Copyright © Alve Jane Aranton

ISBN 9789364945110

All rights reserved.

No part of this publication may be reproduced, transmitted, or stored in a retrieval system, in any form by any means, electronic, mechanical, photocopying, recording or otherwise, without the prior permission of the publisher.

The moral rights of the author have been asserted.

This is a work of fiction. Names, characters, businesses, places, events, locales, and incidents are either the products of the author's imagination or used in a fictitious manner. Any resemblance to actual persons, living or dead, or actual events is purely coincidental.

This book is sold subject to the condition that it shall not by way of trade or otherwise, be lent, resold, hired out or otherwise circulated, without the publisher's prior consent, in any form of binding or cover other than that in which it is published.

www.ukiyoto.com

For the hopeful romantics, dreams do come true.

Contents

Chapter 1	1
Chapter 2	6
Chapter 3	13
Chapter 4	20
Chapter 5	25
Chapter 6	33
Chapter 7	38
Chapter 8	43
Chapter 9	46
Chapter 10	50
About the Author	*52*

Chapter 1
Present

Andy

I know I shouldn't be nervous right now but I couldn't help it, the Barnes & Noble at 5th Avenue where I'm having my first-ever book signing event is packed with people who are anticipating to meet me.

I, the writer, who wrote about a heroine that came out strong amidst life's circumstances. Me, Andy Walter, who had once only dreamed about this whole thing coming into reality.

Me.

There's a reason why I'm best at writing things on paper rather than facing a room full of people just like this. I'm right where I'm supposed to be but it seems I'm never used to all of this attention on me. Honestly, this whole event is nearly making me turn into an anxious puddle on the floor.

Minutes prior the event would start, I find myself reassured that I can confidently face the readers and the press this afternoon. I take in the wide space before me standing behind the makeshift stage in the middle of the bookshop. The sun is shining brightly outside, its golden glow peering in through the glass windows, and the subtle noise of the crowd makes this typical day in New York somehow special. After giving much thought despite all the history in this place, I decided to move in two months ago so I could fully focus on my writing career as advised by my publicist, Trista. I thought that my parents would have doubts of me leaving my hometown but surprisingly, they were supportive of my decision. They couldn't make it today as they're on a retirement trip somewhere in the Caribbean, but we Facetimed early in the morning to send me their well wishes. Although they are far away now, I will never rob them off of the opportunity to see the world together. God knows they have saved up for that trip for so long.

I suddenly hear Trista call my attention with a soft touch on my arm, signaling me that the event would now finally commence. Sporting a polished attire alongside her dominantly red smooth waves cascading down her back, there is still a softness that hangs above her. Nodding, I took a deep breath, wore a smile and made my way to where I should be.

***

Everything went unexpectedly smooth.

I had read out loud a few snippets, spoke to readers and answered a few questions about my book. Being able to speak on writing about a small-town came like a breeze knowing I wrote it with such tender authenticity. That was what my book has been made popularly known for as Trista always reminds me of.

The people who came to the event appeared to be genuinely interested in my output and before I knew it, time went dwindling down towards sunset. I am sitting on a wooden stool where I'm supposed to sign copies of my book. Rolling up my sweater sleeves and pen ready, I whisked my signature away onto every copy bought. The line is somehow long but I'm not at all restless. Women excitedly presented their copies for me to sign and I profusely thanked each of them in gratitude. After having signed numerous copies, I had clumsily let go of my pen and I saw it dropping like a pin onto the floor beneath me. Great, I'm really not used to this whole signing thing and so I picked it up as quickly as possible so as not to keep the person next in line waiting but I was in complete and utter shock after seeing who appeared before me.

A lump in my throat grows that catches me off-guard, stopping me to even make any remark. Nothing ever prepared me for this moment, that I would see him again in the flesh now, in this moment right here, right now. Before this, I used to believe running into him in New York would be impossible but I guess now, it isn't.

Is my mind playing tricks on me or is the world on standstill? Do I feel everyone's eyes like a spotlight or was it his that is boring deeply into my soul?

He towered over me looking handsome, tall and strong just as I had imagined all these years. Eyes a golden hazel, his rolled-up blue button-down shirt looking prim. That easy, warm and comforting smile he always had that was now right in front of me, was the summary of all the past memories that are returning. I could feel my heart pulsating in my head, my palms starting to sweat and I was just simply there unable to say or do something decent. Trying my best to keep my composure, I quickly grabbed the book from his hold so I could avoid touching his skin or looking into his eyes for long.

Ready to sign the pristine page of the book, I heard myself clear my throat and said, "To whom should I dedicate this book for?" I can feel him near, so near, his proximity making me all the more nervous.

"To me..." He gulped and cleared his throat, pausing to say his name out loud, as if I don't know how familiar those four letters are. "Reed. My name's Reed. Uhm, for the book." He points to the blank page, seemingly unsure of himself. Is he as tense as I am? Because he sounds like that. Ignoring the tension surrounding us both, I swiftly signed, wrote a short note and closed his copy of the book. The sooner I finish this, the faster he will move past for the next one in line but no he doesn't seem to disappear out of my sight anytime soon as he looks at me—really looks into my eyes now as if pleading, begging for more time. I wouldn't let him get to me, after what had happened two years ago.

Staring at him, I was certain he was going to say something before finally deciding to leave but instead I simply heard him settle with, "Thank you, Ms. Walter."

And then he's gone.

For the second time around, one of us walks away again.

Chapter 2
Past (Two Years Ago)

Andy

"Andy it's just a dating app. You've got to try it, everyone's doing it right now." Jessie says with utmost enthusiasm to rid me of my annoyance and hesitation while I'm preparing her warm cup of Cappuccino. She's been adamantly pushing me to sign up for one as her constant worry about my non-existent love life is growing more and more. I get it, I'm 25 and should be dating but the closest romantic relationship I have is with a fictional character. Lame as it sounds but the possibility of actually getting to know someone who's genuinely a great guy is close to none because let's get this real, there's no place for hopeless romantics like me in this day and age so why try? I've got bigger goals ahead of me and that is to become a published writer. It's no longer going to cut it if I keep working as a barista in our local coffee shop when I could be doing far greater things. It's a big dream to hope for but it's my creative writing degree, determination and talent that's going to be my edge. And so do many others.

The competition is tougher these days and it's a struggle to keep up. I've been working on another novel that's appearing to be very ambitious for now but I'm keeping my fingers crossed this one's going to end all of the rejection letters. God knows I've had countless of them hidden inside my desk drawer.

It's fifteen minutes before I clock out on a Friday night and my best friend still couldn't keep her mouth shut about her plea. She's waiting for my shift to end so she could sleep over in my tiny apartment like she always seemed to do frequently. Besides, with Jessie's company, you'll never get bored.

Jessie and I met in college in one of our Psychology classes and ever since then we clicked despite our differences. She's outgoing and easy to be with unlike the quiet, introverted girl that is me. Jessie always had boys around her but she only has eyes for one— her boyfriend Ben who's working as an engineer in California. Although they're in a long-distance relationship for a year now, they would always find the time to talk to each other while Jessie is staying here working in Events Planning. My dating track record on the other hand isn't exactly as exciting as hers though.

"Just how trendy is this dating app thing actually? I'm trying to entertain your suggestion so there would be a slight possibility of you shutting up about this whole ordeal." Removing my apron out of me, I said to her.

"Remember Shelly? A friend from work?" I nodded in response to her reply.

"Well, she's been dating this guy for over a year now and she's met him on a dating app. When she told me about it I instantly thought of you! Come on Andy, at least tell me you're open to this idea?"

"Aren't there a lot of creeps in apps like that? Guys only want hook-ups these days." I settle right across from her now to the table she's sitting in. I pulled my long, thick, dark brown hair in a bun, my bag kept to my side and leaned in closely with my arms.

"There could possibly be weirdos there but we'll try to look for someone decent enough, okay?" Jessie's blonde hair is messy and yet it still works. I rolled my eyes at her and smiled. She really doesn't seem to be giving up anytime soon. This is all weird but her concern actually warms my heart.

"Okay, whatever, but let's get to the nearest grocery store first before heading home, shall we?" I shifted the subject as quickly as I could and she seemed to agree with my proposal then.

***

I had just gotten out of the shower in my robe and face mask ready when I saw Jessie sitting comfortably in my bed, holding my phone in her hand. After dinner and some wine, we've decided to watch a movie like we always do but seeing her there engrossed in my phone looks so weird. Please tell me she isn't doing what I think she's doing?

Before I got to her to grab it, she pulled my phone away from me in defense and said, "Promise you won't be mad at me? I just had to do it."

"Oh my gosh, what did you do?" I tried to fight her but she just wouldn't hand me back my cellphone.

"I made you an account and there are a ton of guys who are already waiting for you." That wicked grin on her face always shows up when she's got a wicked plan she so desperately wants to happen. I wanted to scream at her for getting me into any of this. She knows that dating applications aren't exactly my kind of scene but I guess for now I could no longer avoid it knowing she's got it all laid out for me.

And then there it hits me, as I sit beside her on my bed, that although I try to shrug it off, I haven't felt this lonely. My only ever long-term relationship ended a year ago and it lasted for three years. Tom and I remain simply just friends now and because there's this pressure to be an independent woman who goes after her goals, I haven't given dating much thought after that. But it doesn't mean that I don't feel alone because honestly, I do. I wish I had someone to go home to or talk to on an emotional, deeper level other than my best friend. Jessie was right, maybe I should just give this a shot.

She returns my phone for me to see, the bright glare of my phone screen is right before my eyes. Jessie had downloaded an app called *Connect*—a rather cliché name, might I add, that lets singles around the world connect to each other. She had made me a profile stating my age and my job to which she wrote as Writer. I looked at her suspiciously before I chose to see my profile picture but there's a hint of playfulness in her eyes that says she won. Just the thought of thinking about what picture she's chosen made me nervous. I tapped the profile button and my best friend carefully picked a rather presentable picture of me, all smiles with a dash of make-up I took weeks ago. My skin glowed, my eyes were bright and my lips pulled up in a smile. There's no hiding that I'm a woman of color considering my Filipino heritage but it's something that I'm not ashamed of at all. The image Jessie picked in my phone gallery was not as bad as I thought.

"Here are your possible matches." She carefully taps my screen to a heart button somewhere at the far left. She continued to explain that in the matches button, there I can find profiles of guys who pushed my "heart" button on the app waiting for me to tap theirs back so we could be a match. Okay, maybe this wasn't rocket science after all. It's been minutes now since she's gotten me acquainted with the whole thing and warned me to carefully choose who I connect with. "Time to see the guys?" She suggested as she went on. I simply nodded as I went into the matches section.

There are over 10 guys who have tapped me as a possible match but most of them looked like guys who only want to get laid. A display of countless shirtless pictures of men made me want to throw up so Jess and I pushed the X button without any reluctance. Just as I was about to give up, towards the bottom, I see a picture of a guy who without a doubt sparked my interest. I know looks don't matter but seeing him there caught my eye. When I opened his profile I swear I heard Jessie squeal like a high school girl beside me. In the image, I see a 28 year-old Reed, his name calling out to me from the screen. His hair is swept sleek in dark chestnut brown. He's clad in a dress shirt, white coat and a stethoscope slung over his shoulders. From the looks of it, he is a doctor. There is a softness that is painted in his fine demeanor and a genuine, easy smile. I haven't known him yet but he appears to be someone who would most likely do gentlemanly things like open your car door for you or buy you flowers on random occasions. I wondered, if he looks just as attractive as this, why would he even settle for a dating app when he could be meeting someone organically? It's the only one in three pictures I've seen and I'm already being magnetically pulled by this guy.

"Should I?" I asked her as Jessie bobbed her head in agreement. Before I know it, I'm pushing the heart button back so we could be a match. Apparently, Reed is from New York, the only disadvantage that I could see between us early on. "So what if he's in New York?" Jessie retorts back.

"Jessie, I'm literally miles away from this guy. I'm in a small town in Colorado and he's somewhere in a big city. Will this ever work?" I pointed out to her but it seems Jessie always had answers for everything. "Just think of Ben and I. And besides, you're still getting to know this guy who also happens to be very good-looking. See how it goes from there, okay?" She responded and that comforted me a little thus far.

I was staring wide-eyed at his picture for long now although feeling a sudden wave of insecurity come over me. A ping in my phone—a simple hello from Reed that seemed like the beginning of everything—made me and Jess slightly jolt from our seats.

Chapter 3
Present

Andy

St. Jude's Hospital invited over Trista and I for a luncheon benefit on a warm Saturday afternoon as Dr. Ricky Jenkins, head of the Oncology Department, had been kind enough to be my consultant for a new book I'm planning to work on after my debut novel. It's still roughly in the works but I'm trying my hardest not to make the next one a colossal failure. The old man's been very helpful thus far. It's hard to beat a debut and I'm more than determined to outdo my first one. Plus, it's also a great opportunity for me to make a donation for further research and breakthroughs in this department knowing it's close to my heart. My late grandmother died of Breast cancer six years ago and it's one way for me to honor her through this chosen charity.

After the opening ceremony has ended, Dr. Jenkins gladly showed us around to meet with some of the doctors who took part in the event with white wine in hand. Several doctors came to praise me for my book debut and thanked them for their kind words. Trista and I are standing close by together while we're getting to know some of the others when one of them, Dr. Hilton—a guy who's probably in his late thirties said, "Dr. Lockhart was right, the book was good. Biggest fan among all of us!" I wondered who this Dr. Lockhart was when I have this person to thank for as a reader. I still couldn't believe that people would come up to me and say that they loved my work. It's both fascinating and flattering all the same yet it humbles me more.

"Well, we've got to meet Dr. Lockhart if you say so that she's such fan of her work!" Trista replied with amusement.

"She? No, he's a he. He's one of our best surgeons here in St. Jude's." Dr. Hilton replied playfully, looking at me then Trista, far longer. Trista wore a wonderful maroon dress that fell just right above the knees looking like the professional publicist that she is. She was undeniably stunning right now and for a second, I might have noticed Dr. Hilton try to catch her attention for a date. There are sparks everywhere between them that's for sure. "Oh I stand corrected." Trista responded with that subtle twinkle in her eye. Dr. Hilton sips wine from his glass when he suddenly looks behind me and said, "Oh there he is! Dr. Lockhart, you've got to meet your favourite author."

Just when I turn my back to see him, he's already right beside where I am standing and as I looked up, the shock that came over me a week ago at the book signing event started reoccurring however this time, twice the intensity.

So it's Reed. Reed Lockhart. Dr. Reed Lockhart. That's what his full name was. This is the same guy from two years ago—the one I tried forgetting but just couldn't.

This is the same guy I saw without warning at my event last week. This is really him. And he's standing so close I could feel his suit glide over my bare arm. I had not seen our world shrink even smaller so soon. Not once did I see this coming.

I couldn't bring myself to make a move when he's looking down on me with a growing passion in his gaze. He's tall and wonderfully dressed in a suit and tie. I feel all eyes on me again but maybe I'm just overthinking things. He wakes me up from my trance all of a sudden when he offers his hand for me to shake. "Nice to meet you *again* in person, Ms. Walter." He said with a voice that's both deep and velvety.

I take his strong hand into mine, "Please, just call me Andy." I'm afraid to grip his hand for long so I quickly let go afterward. There's an awkward silence in the air that everyone could have possibly felt by now. "Well okay, maybe we should let you two speak then." Dr. Hilton suggested as he disappeared with Trista. Great, we're all alone now. I'm fidgeting while he's kept his hands in his pockets the whole time. If we had just been typical good old friends maybe this wouldn't have been so uncomfortable but getting involved with him two years ago, strangely, on a dating app? This makes things all the more unconventional.

I tried to break the tension and said, "So, you work here now?" I look up at him, holding my wineglass every so tightly. "Yeah, I matched here for my residency. Remember when I was… never mind." He replied but I feel his entire sentence fade away knowing it's dangerous territory to normalize our past. To be honest, I'm not ready to reconnect with him, in person now, after two years. If we stick to small talk then this entire conversation would be tolerable. He's standing not too close and not too far from me. I am starting to see him fully and truly. I won't deny myself of the fact that he's beautiful standing over there. Like he's confident and sure of himself; like he knows exactly what he's doing.

"I'm glad about that. That you're here now. I mean, now that you're a surgeon, it's a thing to be proud of." I said to him, taking a peek into his eyes.

"I'm happy for you too. It's a wonderful book, what you have written." He replied with a sincerity in his voice. Another surge of awkwardness surrounded us both where we're standing and none of us were ever sure who's going to speak again first.

"Look, Reed." I finally said, uttering his name out loud for the first time in years and continued, "that time during my book singing— it really surprised me. I honestly haven't thought about ever seeing you.. again."

"It was the only way that I could personally meet my favourite writer. The only way I could meet you." He sheepishly smiled, rubbing his hand to his neck.

"Stop.. Please don't say things like that." I said, stopping him, ignoring the butterflies tingling in the pit of my stomach.

He replied, eyebrows furrowing, surprised. "What do you mean?" He started moving in a step closer to me.

"Stop making it seem like things are… alright between us." I said so in a hushed voice for the unsuspecting people around us.

"I know it's been two years but will you ever give me a chance to explain?" It's like every word he's saying is a move nearer towards me. My heart's growing wearier and more nervous by the minute.

"I would let you but here's the thing, Reed—it's like I know you but I also don't." I said with disappointment because that's the truth, I know a lot about him and yet he's also this big stranger to me.

"I understand that. It's just that what happened two years ago.. I couldn't let go of it so easily, you know?" He says with a quiet ease despite the grimness of our conversation. For a second I wanted to agree with him—that what we had wasn't something so easily to let go of but then I had to choose the healthier option for him and mostly for myself. I didn't deserve any of it.

"Do I hear regret in your voice? I remember you told me handling regret wasn't something you've fully mastered to do. I can see it 'til now." I snarled at him rather softly but I know my words were sounding bitter. I sensed the discomfort in his face and for a second I wanted to take back what I had said. Have I been too harsh on him?

Just when he decided to respond to my cruel words, he was stopped by a woman grabbing his arm from behind and in it came a blonde woman with the bluest eyes I've seen, holding him like she wouldn't let him go. She had a slim figure and statuesque height, an aura of some old classic film star. Looking at them side by side was like staring at a picture perfect magazine cover. I gulped with how oddly things have turned. Was this woman his girlfriend?

I hear her clear her throat and introduced herself. "Oh it's our beloved guest, celebrated author. Hello Ms. Walter. It's nice to meet you." She raised her hand for a handshake. "I'm Dr. Rachel Jenkins, Dr. Ricky's daughter, we are so happy to have you here this afternoon."

"Oh my thank you." I plastered on a smile that wasn't too obviously fake and reached for her hand. "Well it's an honor. I'm looking forward to making donations this year. It's my chosen charity after all and well your father has helped me a lot for the next book I'm writing about." God does she smile so eerily wide and Reed is so uncomfortable standing there with her. What I'd do to find Trista so we could leave sooner.

The she giggled. A giggle? Really? And touched Reed's arm lightly. "Dr. Lockhart and I were just speaking about how I went about writing with my debut novel seeing he's such a big fan." I told her trying to snap Reed's attention back to Rachel's as he was casually either staring down at me or at his shoes.

"Yes, my boyfriend's a big fan of your work." There she said it, with blinking eyes and batting eyelashes while here I am in a usual position, discovering a fact I'm always just the last to know. A waitress holding her tray up was coming by me and I just had to carefully place my empty wine glass back in before I accidentally broke it. I feel the temperature rise a bit in the function hall and each second that ticks by makes me want to run away but instead I faked a smile and pinned my eyes solely on Reed who could no longer turn his glance on me. "Well I should probably get going. I have an appointment with my publisher at 4. Trista and I wouldn't miss it for the world." Then, I sashayed myself away in the smoothest way possible when I hear Reed call me out for the last time. "Wait—Andy, will I see you again?" I turned to face him, his question crawling down my back. "Our world has just gotten way smaller, Dr. Lockhart." With a smrik, I left both of them be.

Chapter 4
Past (Two Years Ago)

Andy

"I'll tell you a secret." I see Reed through the screen sitting comfortably in his study desk, his face glowing despite the long day he's had. He's been through a long day full of lectures and studying for his final US-MLE before he's going to become a resident. The struggles and anxieties he's dealt with for the past few years to become a doctor aren't easy to shrug off that's why I'm doing my best to just hear him out and be there for him. It's what he needs most. New York hasn't been all sunshine and smiles for him lately, as he always says. "I listened to JLO at the gym today and tell ya, it pumped me up." I laughed at his revelation when I told him I secretly keep an early 2000s pop playlist somewhere in my phone for days when I just need to feel good.

It's been two months since Reed and I were talking over this app that Jessie put me in and so far it's been great. It's my favourite time of the day when we would sit down and talk about even the most random to the personal stuff over chat, voice mail or like this one, a video call. I found this connection with Reed I haven't found with anyone else, not even with Tom. It's like we just get lost in the conversations. He would even send me a long list of songs he'd like me to listen to and I'd do the same; he would tell me how his days would go; how they've moved from Europe to America when he was just young; how his grandmother would bring him daisies, his favourite flower, as a child; how he's close to his grandparents; how he wanted so much to become a doctor because of his grandfather; how vulnerable he is and knows it yet isn't afraid to do so with me. How could a man like Reed exist in this world and yet is living far away?

I zoned out for a second there looking at him and admiring his angelic features while here I am, ordinary as can be. "Our time difference's pretty significant." He said, as I carefully swiped on a lipstick, getting ready for work, near my vanity. Raising his arms at the back of his head, he just studied me for a moment—feeling slightly self-conscious, I turned to look at him. Behind him, I could see a glimpse of his room. It's white, not much stuff anywhere but his big, soft bed, a bedside lamp beside it and a desk full of books, readings and pens. "Just when I'm about to go to bed, your day's just starting."

"I know. I practically live in the future." I replied playfully, moving closer to the screen on my phone so he could clearly look at me. Without a doubt we seem to flirt a lot but it's still unclear what our label really is. It confuses the hell out of me but I'm scared of bringing it up to him. The last thing I want is to scare him away.

"What's it like in the future anyway?" He asked, leaning in closer with his harms on the desk, his biceps showing through his dark shirt.

"It's just as wonderful as you hope it would be." I resorted to the safest answer because I badly wanted to tell him I want to be a part of that future he's asking me. I want his summers and winters and all moments, big or small with him, but I couldn't tell him that just yet. We were staring in each other's eyes now without saying anything and I feel my heart beat through my white shirt. The tension growing between us is undeniably present.

"You know what, it's your warm smile that really got me to you?" He revealed and it took me by surprise, a dimple showing in his left cheek. Compliments from him really turn me into a rock. I smiled at the thought of him thinking about my smile. "Yup, there it is." I feel blood rushing to my face, his observation making me weak in the knees.

"Okay honesty time." I urged him and he went in to listen closely. "I just wanted to ask but if you don't want to answer—"

"No, ask away and I'll tell you with full disclosure." He said.

"Well, I was wondering if you were speaking to somebody else other than me? Just to set things straight." I bit my lip, nervous to what his answer was going to be.

"I was talking to other people." He slowly said, and I feel my stomach drop. "Oh okay." I replied looking down, the silence suddenly hitting us both.

"Did this just suddenly change the whole environment of our conversation?" He asked, brow raising in question.

"No, no it's just—" I argued. "Ugh, I ruined it, didn't I?" Sensing my own frustration, I covered my face in shame.

"No, you didn't, Andy. You absolutely didn't." He said with a smirk on his face. "I have been talking to other people but I realized how distracted I got."

"Am I distracting you, though? I hope I'm not steering you clear away from your goals." I interrupted him, feeling myself getting a little uneasy and furious.

"You're not a distraction, Andy." I hear him huff a breath, reassuring me. "In fact, this, is a quiet refuge to my daily stresses. This calms me down a lot." His eyes bore into me so deep that I could no longer feel the screen between us. If I could just kiss him, I would. "And it's just you, no one else." Just me. No one else. Just as I was with him. I felt his words resounding like an echo, one I didn't want to fade into nothingness.

I cleared my throat to break the intensity growing between us. "This really calms me down too. A hell lot." I agreed, and his lips turn up into a shy smile. I looked down on my hands but I can feel him just watching me through the screen. Snapping back into reality, I checked out the time so I could rush to work.

"Hey, Reed? I'm gonna have to work now. Good night where you are?" I said so with the hope and certainty that he'll still be there tomorrow. He seemed to understand and decided to move away from the screen until I hear him catch up to ask me, "Are we good though, Andy?"

There is a tinge of worry in his voice I couldn't exactly put my finger on and I nodded, smiled at him just so in reassurance, before saying goodbye.

Chapter 5
Present

Weeks have gone by and there was no sign of Reed near me. After meeting him multiple times, it made me recall the past and it simply wasn't helpful. I'd rather he and I go into opposite directions, far from each other as much as possible than our worlds gravitating even more closely. I've been telling Jessie all about what's been happening to me when we Facetime as much as we could, and while she was curious, she simply allowed me to react the way I should. She knew it all and witnessed what a mess I've made of myself two years prior and even with my recent experience, she still was the same person I could turn to no matter what. I've grown so much in the past years but when it comes to matters of the heart, I couldn't help but admit that I'm stuck somewhere in the middle, far from Jessie who's now in California with Ben. Jessie decided to finally make the big move with him and even when it was a huge leap, it was a step she knew was worth taking, and as her best friend, I couldn't be any happier.

I have been deeply committed to finishing several chapters of the book I'm currently working on. If being in my pyjamas for days on end, hair a mess in front of the computer, and standing up for a few minutes or so to look at the Manhattan sunset after a long day of writing was close to being productive then yes, I think

I made the cut. It was all fun and games until I realized I was beginning to feel stuffy for being stuck in the apartment this long. Trista believed I should go out more often and more importantly, get myself back out there, dating like any normal twenty-something should. I've had a couple of dates and flings over the years but none of them were close to anything serious or long-term and I preferred to keep it that way.

When my writing career started taking off, I knew I had to pour my focus and attention to it and saw how this opportunity was something I needed to last a lifetime. Yet here I am, finding myself getting dressed up for a date Trista had set me up with. I was nervous and slightly hesitant but I didn't want to disappoint her and besides, maybe I could try to get back out there. It wouldn't hurt to deal with small talk and ice breakers yet again, right?

We had dinner at a posh restaurant called *Eleven Madison Park*. It was romantic and well-lit and sitting across from me was my date James, who Trista set me up with. He is an accountant, that looked like a rich white frat boy. He seemed relaxed and cool, confident, as though he knew for sure how the night was going to be like for us. But James, tall and attractive as he is-- blonde and blue eyes, still felt like a person that resembled an afterthought. There was nothing mesmerizing about him that captivated me but still, I tried hard to keep the conversation flowing just so we could part ways and call it a good night.

When I made an excuse to meet a friend for drinks, he took it as a sign that I didn't want to go as he had planned, so he ended up kissing my cheek softly and we parted ways eventually. I felt terrible for lying to him but I wanted to spend some time alone and get a drink so I turned my way to walk a few blocks and found a quiet bar.

The place wasn't as occupied as it should be and I took a spot at the center of its u-shaped bar and wraparound counter seating. The music was turned low and I got a few drinks to don on my own, sitting just comfortably in solitude, in a black dress that didn't feel like me at all. I sense someone taking a spot beside me, occupying my peripheral vision. I turned to see who that was so I could move a little but I was surprised to see it was Reed.

Reed was a good inches away from me and he was as shocked as I was. He looked exhausted from a long day's work as it appeared. His button-down rolled up, veins in the arms peeking through and his cheeks a red flush. I didn't know what exactly to say. I wasn't sure if I uttered a casual hi or friendly hello but I knew he spoke and broke the tension first. "Andy I.. I didn't expect to see you again." He said so honestly and I couldn't agree more. "Me either, I just-- wow, has the world gone stranger everyday?" I replied, in a disappointing sigh.

"For bumping into me again?" He asked.

"I mean, we both are in New York so how is that any different? It shouldn't feel weird. " I wondered, tipsy and cheeks getting warmer.

"It's different if one of the two people who used to know each other, now hates seeing the other person around." He said, in a voice so low and seemingly hard to make out of yet I still heard him.

For a few minutes or so, we sat in silence, just drinking until he spoke up again to get rid of the awkwardness.

"You're in here alone?" He asked as he now turned towards me.

"Yes. I was just on a date a few hours ago and--"

"And it didn't go well?" I could hear his curiosity along with his close proximity to me.

"It did go well. Just didn't feel like I could handle another round of it." I replied, my mouth pursed in disappointment.

"Ah, I see. One of those boring ol' dates, huh?"

"Yeah, one of those boring ol' dates." I said so in subtle sarcasm. "What about you? Long day?"

"Long ass day. Patient rounds, surgery. It's been pretty hectic that I could sleep on this stool bar anytime now." He expressed and gave off a little laugh. I laughed a bit too, just so in consolation because I felt how tired he was. Having demanding work hours was the typical life of a doctor and I knew it then when he was still studying for it. Even more so now that he's one, I still felt the pressure just as it was. He used to tell me a lot about his days and when I sensed it felt familiar somehow just as he did, I retreated back with silence. Suddenly, so many thoughts of him came to visit. My brain was now filled to the brim and yet I couldn't let them out. I just continued to drink and felt tipsier than earlier. Trying to hide the embarrassment I felt for my low tolerance, I stood up, almost tripping on my heels when Reed caught ahold of me.

"Andy, I don't think you should go home alone." I removed my arm from his grasp and fixed my hair as I rudely said to him, "Okay well, should I have some guy with me then?" I honestly wasn't completely attuned with myself now and I felt guilty about retorting back to him this way.

I felt him fall silent but he stood up and grabbed his coat, ready to hold my arm softly again. "I'll take you home, we'll get a cab together and I promise, you'll be there in a minute, unscathed." I could feel the warm air of his breath so near me and I almost tried to fight my way. My head was both empty and full yet here I was, willfully allowing myself to get pulled by the chaos that was him again.

The entire cab ride was a moment of silence between us where the noise of the engine and busy streets only surrounded us both. I asked Reed to stop us a few blocks away from my apartment so I could clear my head and get some air. Thankfully he agreed on the off-chance that I let him walk with me just to get me home safe.

The air was turning chilly as the night went on and we slowly walked our way through. His tall build towered over me as we paced through and I caught tiny glimpses of his face to look at how he was doing. "She wouldn't bother you being with me here tonight, I hope?" I asked in reassurance and we found ourselves stopping for a moment. His face was beautiful and gentle under the streetlights as he turned to stare at me. I sensed the stress catching up on him as he rubbed his neck and sighed a heavy sigh I haven't heard in a long time.

"Andy, I'm... you should know I'm terribly sorry for--" He uttered and I didn't want to hear what was going to follow that.

"No, don't go there again, Reed. Don't take me back there." I raised my hands in defense, as if protecting me from someone who could do me wrong. I was on a roll tonight, blurting out words that didn't seem like things I would say out loud. I was stupid and terrible and I wouldn't blame him if he'd leave me in the middle of this lonely, dark street. He stepped on his other leg, loosened a button on his shirt and let out a breath.

"What could I possibly do, Andy? Please get me to wrap my head around it so I could figure you out." His voice was growing deeper and louder as he looked down on me. "I just-- am sorry." He said in a mixture of frustration and remorse.

I stepped a few steps back, creating a gap between us and I just stood slightly far from him, with a tear in my eye. *Andy, don't you cry now, you're just drunk*, I thought but all I wanted was to lash out in my misery. He tried to step closer now with every step I take farther back, the streetlights still glancing down on him. He held my arms in a way that burned, his face close enough to mine and I let go, little by little so I could speak. "I wish I could tell you how I feel so clearly, Reed." I sniffed back tears, his hands wiping a tear down from me. I stepped away ever so slightly yet again.

"My heart was filled with so much of you, you know? It's been a house or a place that you've occupied in like a huge box and I.. I still have that box here." I said, pointing to my chest as if making a coherent point. "I want to get rid of it, throw it all away like I should've a long time ago but I couldn't… I just couldn't dare to." His gaze held on to me so intensely as his eyes were on the verge of tears too. "So I… keep that box somewhere, just in case. And I try.. Try again to open up and make space for someone new. Because maybe this time it works." He holds my face and puts his forehead on mine, whispering apologies I wanted badly to hear from him before.

I held his hands as I let myself cry and continued, "Maybe the next person I allow to let in would make this all go away but they just don't. I try and try and I fail every single time." I held his big hands in one tight grasp until I let it fall.

"It's been hard to see you again let alone talk to you after two years." We were both in tears now. I continued, "after you, I've been nothing but changed."

As much as I'd like for him to take me home, I left him there, under the streetlights, all on his own.

Chapter 6
Past (two years ago)

Andy

It's been nearly a year of being with him on the phone every single day. We'd call, text and even go on long video calls since the day we virtually met. I'd watch him pour himself reading and studying. He'd beg to read my work no matter how terrible and amateur my unfinished novels were. I'd keep him awake and send him voice mails on days when he needs a piece of me he could play and return to. Even with differing time zones, we still managed to seemingly make it work. It was the only part of my day where everything made perfect sense despite the banality of my life. Reed really was nothing short of wonderful. He was my person who unfortunately lived miles away. So close yet still so, so very far from me. Someone who knew me just as well as I was with him, and yet he was nowhere near.

But even then, there still was a part of me that was uncertain about all this, about us. Because what are we, really? Good ol' pals who talk to each other everyday with no labels on? Friends who make promises and plans for the future? Friends who say and do as what lovers do? Friends who know each other so well that the screen was nothing but a thin barrier drawn by the universe? Was I really just okay with settling for all that? Whenever those thoughts enter my head, I can't help but feel nervous and uncomfortable. I feel a sudden ache and a longing stretching far all the way to New York. So I decided to finally talk it out with him as far as honesty goes. It's the weekend and we haven't talked in two days because of some very crucial test he had to study for and take in preparation for his USMLE. Just nearly a month away and he'll be on his final step so he could finally get accepted into his Residency program. I've missed him, but duty calls and life always gets in the way.

I sat on my wooden chair, dressed in one of my worn-out shirts, waiting for him. But strangely, as I looked into our stream of conversations, I noticed it was all gone. There was just a wide blank space of nothingness left in there and it made me sit right up. My heart was beating quickly now. Carefully touching the screen, I made sure that I didn't do anything wrong at all. Did he do this on purpose or was the internet just cranky at this hour? Did I do anything wrong that could have set him off? I tried to retrace what happened but nothing seemed to justify it. We were in our usual element from our last conversation, even made plans of where he'd take me to New York when I would finally go there and see him yet here we are.

I waited for a few minutes or so and finally, he did come around. I feel myself loosen up as he was here again. Maybe I was just being paranoid and corrected myself for feeling so.

Hey, sorry. I got caught up so late to the hospital. Forgot my wallet and my keys so I had to catch the ferry on the way to Hudson. He typed in and I understood him, reassured that it was all okay.

Oh, no worries. I totally understand. You're good though? I replied.

Yes, sure. He typed back with a response so dull that it seemed to appear so strange. It was unlike him to have a tone just like that.

Okay, can we talk? I wanted to ask you about something. Should we just text or call then? Just let me know okay, I know you've had a long day. I typed nervously and it took him quite a bit to respond.

I heard a ping from my phone a little later.

Actually, I've been meaning to tell you this, Andy. Just out of honesty, I am in a relationship. His response was so straightforward that it didn't give me a second or two to wrap my head around it. My hands were shaking ever so slightly now trying to figure out the words he said right back at me.

What do you mean? Reed, you can't be kidding right now. What's gotten into you? Are you okay? I wanted so badly to call him but I don't think he didn't want to hear from me at all. **Are you serious? Your girlfriend knows about us?**

She does. She's actually coming back home.

She's home from where?

Studying abroad... Reed was direct and quick as if wanting to get rid of me was the only thing he wanted to do today.

This started out as a joke. I'm sorry, Andy. I didn't mean to go far around this long. I never knew you'd be this wonderful, so I stayed. Because of you. He replied and little by little, I'm wasting away, hurting inside. This could not possibly be real. He hadn't brought this up for the long time we were speaking. Or was I the one who read this all wrong? Did I not ask the right questions at the beginning to miss out on this earth-shattering information?

My mind was all over the place. I didn't know what it was that really hurt now-- the thought of him breaking this all to me or the fact that I'm the *other* girl without my knowledge. I felt pure disgust coming over me, my skin crawling with dishonesty and hurt.

What have we been doing all this time? Has a prank ever existed this long directed to a nobody like me? I feel my tears coming, one warm tear after another. I crawled into bed and knelt, covering my face with my hands as I let out a silent cry in the small bedroom of my apartment, careful I would even make a sound. I cried and cried out of the pain and embarrassment that crushed me in an instant. How could the person you once knew so well turn into a stranger, just like that? In one big surprise, it's like I lost all of him altogether.

And so I did what I did best and deleted everything there ever was so he wouldn't ever reach me again. If he could disappear with a roaring revelation, I knew the only way to bow out of the scene was to leave him reeling from my silence.

Chapter 7

Present

Several weeks have gone and passed after my encounter with Reed and I've been doing my best at holding up just fine. It was dangerous being around him like that. My emotions really got the best of me. Recalling that blurry night, I have only just ever been honest. Maybe just so, a little too much.

My book is close to publishing after a pouring hours and days of work. I have the final manuscript and as courtesy, I've gotten copies for my consultants so they could have a firsthand glance before it's printed out. Surely, Dr. Jenkins was one of them. He'd been a great help and I wanted to personally thank him for his help and contribution.

After having lunch with Trista, I headed straight to St. Jude's Hospital to hand it over to Dr. Jenkins' office. The day was beautifully warm and sunny-- a wonderful time to take a walk down to the hospital in the middle of fast-paced New York. What busy people they are in this side of the world, working to the bone, catching up on the next train and cab. But despite that, I liked the normalcy of it. Normal yet seemingly lonely.

Before I know it, I reached his assistant's desk. Unfortunately, he was on rounds and had an unexpected meeting later that afternoon, so I simply handed the manila envelope that was my manuscript. I thanked his assistant and went on towards my way out. As I was walking casually, I heard heels clacking behind me fast. I heard a woman's voice that was so familiar, simply calling out for my name. I turned to look behind me and there was Rachel. Good, not another encounter with the last person I don't want to talk to. I paused and waited for her to reach me. She seemed like she was off-duty, her blonde hair was perfect, her legs long in those trouser pants as she approached me with a smile.

"Hey, Andy." Her voice was silky smooth, emphasizing my name as though she needed something. I smiled back and said hello in return. "I just came to send your dad my manuscript. My next book's going to be released next month but it turned out he was busy so.."

"Oh yes. Well, congratulations about that. I'm sure it's going to be just as wonderful as the first." She complimented me and I shyly pulled up a tiny smile. "Anyway, I was going out for coffee. Would you like to join me?" Out of one of the corridors I caught a glimpse of Reed who was oblivious as we were there. He was standing over far, looking at a chart so seriously. His eyebrows burrowing, eyes focused and I stared for a moment or two until he continued walking farther off. I wanted to run and make a terrible excuse so I could leave now but I was cornered and so I ended up agreeing to go join her instead.

Nothing irks me more than small talk. And for the last 30 minutes that I'm sitting across Rachel, our conversations were nothing but the weather, college degree and summer vacations. I took a sip of my latte and tried to keep the ball rolling until I sensed Rachel stiffly sit up, her hands clasped together on the wooden desk as though she were to say something serious. So I sat right up straight as well, mirroring her move.

"Andy, I know about you and Reed." For a second that I've taken a look into her, her voice was not suspicious but rather sympathetic.

"I'm sorry, what? What is it you know about?" I wondered and asked her right back. I'm pretty sure there was no one else who knew about us. Apart from Jessie, it was just me and him, no one else.

"Even two years ago, I knew about you and him." She said, looking down from time to time.

I rested my back on the chair and sighed. "Look, whatever he said, that was-- everything happened two years ago and I'm not here to meddle with both of your lives."

"No, I was there.." She responded, as she bit her lip nervously. "I was the one who messaged you." My mouth slightly opened, in pure utter shock. "What?"

"Two days? He was gone for two days for the simulation test we were having for the USMLE. I've gotten home from London and decided I'd take the test with him. We've been broken up for so long. He was hesitant about having me over but he ended up doing so, as a way to help me until I found my own place." She gulped for a moment to continue and I just sat there, unable to meet her in the eye. "He told me all about you and I didn't like the idea of him moving on, let alone with someone who was so far away. He was in the shower and I borrowed his phone to call my dad but I saw your message there and I--"

"You wrote those to me?" My voice was pitch louder. I was in disbelief about everything I'm hearing right now, two years too late. But somehow, it felt like two years ago was just yesterday.

"I'm so, so sorry, Andy. I tried to find you but couldn't and now you're here I just had to say it after all those years." Her voice sounded like a whisper so the other persons next to us wouldn't hear. "I saw how he wanted so much to be with you. He was looking forward to it, you know? And I didn't want him distracted, what with all the goals he set out for."

"No, you didn't want him distracted, Rachel. You wanted me out of his life and you so effortlessly did." I fought the tears catching up in my throat now. I didn't want to cause a scene nor did I have the strength to and so I just sat there, for a moment or so, watching her unveil the truth.

"He got so angry with me and I tried to make it up. Even after all these years, I just know he's resented me so much. When he saw you again, there was not a day that he had reminded me of what I did." She declared with sadness and discontent, realizing just how terrible that must have been for her to stick through with someone who was a living ghost. "He's always been different with you and I could never be you. He wasn't and will never be like how he is with you, when he's with me."

"I'm so profusely sorry, Andy. I do." She said, trying to reach for my hand but I couldn't dare to. "If you think about it, we're just very much alike. We just love one person differently. And I loved him too, I did." Her long nails dug into her knuckles, with her jewelry and pretty clothes suddenly appearing ugly right in front of me.

"No, Rachel, we're nothing alike." I stood up, pulled my bag and left a bill on the table. "Because I would never intend to hurt someone just like you."

Chapter 8
Present

When Rachel finally spoke to me, I couldn't fully describe the entirety of my situation and feelings. All I knew was that I was confused and still just as hurt. The truth felt so disfigured now, stretched on for far too long and while it was a little glimmer of hope, I could not take back the fact that both me and Reed were suffering from the consequences of that lie. I wallowed in my room for days, taking longer and warmer showers, just allowing myself to grieve for all that was. I wanted to talk to Reed, to reach out but I was shameful and unprepared. I don't think I'm ever ready just yet. Not so soon.

I held on and embraced myself in comfort and forgiveness to the hurt I inflicted. I looked at the Manhattan sunset outside my window and remembered those small moments I wished long ago for Reed and I to stare at the same sunset one day. I realized I loved him. Still. That's why I'm here, remaining immobile from the past. But I know, as the days grow, that there is no one else I should love more but me.

Trista threw me a party for my successful book release in a modern and sophisticated function hall inside an a swanky restaurant called *L'Artusi*. The place was adorned with pretty lights and in it were several invited guests who I had the pleasure of meeting. My publisher and consultants were there, enjoying the glass of champagne being served. While enjoying a glass of my own, I secretly wanted to hide behind in a corner to sit my tired legs down from walking around these heels all night. The night was also getting late but the party has just begun.

I sipped the night away, trying to relax, when I noticed someone tapping me on the shoulder. To my surprise as I turned, there was Reed, beautiful in a tux that fit him so well. His hair slicked back with tulips in his hand, staring into my eyes with a softness that I've always come to know.

"They say tulips represent peace and forgiveness." He holds them and hands them over to me gently. "The kind of flowers you give to someone you have to say sorry for." He said and I grabbed them, smelling just the sweetness it brought. I gave him a soft smile and said, "Thank you Reed, you didn't have to."

"It's your book release after all, I didn't want to come here empty handed." He put his hands in his pockets so smoothly and attractively and there I was madly, head over heels for how he looked tonight. I felt self-conscious, my cheeks blushing, as I was feeling nothing but ordinary. "You look beautiful, by the way." He complimented, and looked down nervously at his feet.

I led Reed to a booth that was more quiet than the rest of the room and we just stood there, looking over at the crowd. "Rachel talked to me about everything."

"Yeah, I was surprised she'd do that." He held his hands together and looked right at me now. "I'm sorry, for what I put you through. It's just been tough on my part to reach out after how long." I listened to him saying those words nervously and gave him the chance to talk.

Opening his palm, I drew in small circles and gentle strokes, a gesture so intimate and yet was something I've always wanted to do to ease his nerves. "Would it be possible that for tonight, we just talk and think about the present?" He held my hand now, his grasp warm and secure, just as I had imagined all this time.

The night went on, with the crowds coasting through the party and with every subtle step, we left to find a space of our own-- unbeknown to all the guests around.

Chapter 9

I woke up with the sight of Reed making breakfast. His white undershirt and shorts in view, busy and engrossed at preparing coffee and cooking eggs in my kitchen. In my own apartment. Where we'd gone after the party and talked for hours through the night. I sat up, hair a mess and still just as groggy.

I walked into the kitchen, timidly just so he would barely notice but he caught me yet again, as I was making my way to him. "Trust me, nobody wakes up pretty." I said in defense, embarrassed about how I looked first thing in the morning. He smiled a smile so wide I swore it reached his ear and began to put the food and coffee on the table. Something about the domestic nature of it all made my stomach do somersaults but I shrugged the idea anyway.

"You look great, Andy. Come, sit." He invited me over and pulled up a chair for me then we took silent bites and sips of our coffee he made for us both. My tiny kitchen was facing the wide window of my apartment overlooking the city and there we were just sitting in comfortable silence, a happiness so warm and full I felt it take over.

"I couldn't remember how many times I've wanted this to happen." He turned to me, after putting his coffee mug down. His eyes were bright, reminiscing. "When you said you'd come to New York one day or when we'd talk about getting to meet halfway, anywhere we could find ourselves in, not a single day has passed when I hadn't thought about this happening and now it has." I smiled at the thought of him saying that, recalling that I did think of it just the same. How badly we longed for each other and now we're here. We paused and just looked straight ahead through the window, savoring such a sacred moment.

"So you and Rachel, what now?" I didn't want to bring this one up but still, I had to.

"I wanted to make peace with the fact that it would never work. Gladly we finally came into an agreement." He said intently, his body pointed towards my direction. "It was so hard for me to deal with what happened with us, Andy. I could've manned up but I was an asshole for not even trying to reach you. You were just gone without any trace. An email was the only thing I got but even with that I didn't even have the face to send you one, not even a message." He explained, remorseful, and I just sat there, listening to him.

"Can you please tell me, what really happened? I knew about it from Rachel but I want to hear it from you too." I pleaded softly and covered his hand with mine.

"She snuck through my phone and shit went down fast. I tried to stop her, yelled at her afterwards that I couldn't imagine being that mad over something or someone yet there I was." His shoulders hung low, his voice apologetic and regretful. "I've been so anxious about my future that when she reminded me of the last shot I had with the test, I just let things end up like that. But inside, I felt terrible as hell for what happened to you. Not a day went by where I didn't think of you. I still have the list of your songs on my phone. Your old work, I kept in a folder in my laptop. Your pictures. Your soft smile that I have tucked inside my head. Every little piece of you? Still with me. " His eyes were tearful and he was trying to fight them back.

"I could've been there with you, you know? I would have stayed with you right there, no matter where you were at that point in your life." I responded, my cheeks burning, warm. "I was just so hurt by it. So unimaginably hurt. I don't think I've ever had that much sadness and regret over someone. But then again, I was wrong too, for just leaving like that."

We were quiet for a moment, until Reed responded. "No, I understand. I wouldn't blame you at all. Those were such terrible things to send to a person and I would've been just devastated." His voice was low and there was a hint of dismay there.

"It is cowardly of me to admit that I remained because I owe a lot to Rachel's dad. But before I even saw you in New York, I knew there was only one person who took up a space just right here." He held my hand and placed it over his chest, where I felt his heart beat swiftly. "I did try just like you but trying to believe I was in love with someone else was a lie I've lived through a thousand times."

I felt a tear falling down as so did his too then he pulled me on top of him so I could sit on his lap. Like muscle memory, I wrapped my arms around him. "Can I kiss you, Andy?" And with a little nod I let him and his kiss wiped the tears away. His mouth was gentle on mine, careful and reassuring. I broke away from the kiss, hung up on the intensity of the passion.

"I don't know if I want to pick up where we left off so soon." I said with honesty and a little bit of hesitation because I didn't want to rush things just as it was slowly coming together. He looked at my eyes with an understanding of those words. "But I know that we can always start over again." I smiled and he did too and for once in a long time, things started to make perfect sense.

Chapter 10

9 months Later

Reed and I have remained really good friends. After reconnecting, he went to move to Seattle for his 10-month fellowship at Grace Hospital. We haven't talked that much but we still do, from time to time. I figured and decided I needed to heal from all of it and it helped that we both agreed we had a lot of growing up to do. I miss his presence sometimes but it was all a part of our decision-- one me and him had to live through.

Jessie's wedding reception is nearly ending and we're all just waiting for them to take off to their honeymoon. My legs were tired and although my silky blue dress looked pretty, I wanted nothing more but to change into much more comfortable clothes. I've never seen Jessie and Ben happier than tonight and my heart warmed just by looking at them. They made it and they've got the rest of their lives to make it.

We were all waiting at the entrance of the pavilion where the reception took place to witness the newlyweds being sent off to Paris. Just a few minutes and I'll watch Jessie take on a new chapter of her life. She bid goodbye to the guests but most of all, particularly stopped by me so she could pull me in a tight hug. I tried to fight back the tears as I embraced her even tighter. "Have a wonderful time in Paris. And promise, you'll send pictures." I said and we giddily hugged each other for one more time. With the car honking at her, she gave a final squeeze in my hand and whispered into my ear, "and promise me, this time, you'll give yourself a shot at happiness." I wondered at a cryptic message but she turned to look at someone behind me and pointed, so I could follow her gaze. And then there was Reed, coming through the willow tree decorated in fairy lights as I opened my mouth in surprise. Before I could process what was happening, Jessie and Ben took off while Reed was making his way to me.

"Did she plan all this?" I asked, confused with it all, as he reached for me closer now. "But aren't you in Seattle or something?"

He nodded, with a playful smile forming on his mouth."Oh I flew so I could help a best friend out make her best friend happy." He bit his lip and rubbed his neck-- a movement I've put in memory when he's somehow nervous or unsure about what he was going to do. He now offered his hand for me to take and I did, both hands seemingly perfectly fit like a puzzle piece.

"So, should we pick up right where we left off?" He asked, as we were slowly walking now. "Oh, absolutely." I said so in response, smiling up to meet his eyes. The night was long but it was ours and there we were, allowing our feet to where it may lead us.

About the Author

Alve Jane Aranton

Alve is a 29-year-old Filipino writer who loves to weave dreams into words. From magazines to online brands, she has crafted writings that inspire. With each passion project, Alve proves dreams do come true.

www.ingramcontent.com/pod-product-compliance
Lightning Source LLC
LaVergne TN
LVHW041636070526
838199LV00052B/3388